For MY mama.
-DC

Published by blue manatee press, Cincinnati, Ohio.
blue manatee press and associated logo
are registered trademarks of Arete Ventures, LLC.

First Edition: April 2019.

Library of Congress Cataloging-In-Publication Data
My Mama Is a Mechanic / by Doug Cenko—1st ed.
Summary: Snuggle with Mom for this sweet book about a mother as seen through her son's
eyes. To him, she is a surgeon when she repairs his favorite stuffed animal, a chemist when in the
kitchen, and an architect when they play with toy blocks. But no matter what happens, she is al-
ways his mama, and that's the most important thing of all!
ISBN-13 (hardcover): 978-1-936669-71-4
[Juvenile Fiction — Imagination & Play. 2. Juvenile Fiction — Family/Parents.]
Printed in the USA.

MY MAMA IS A Mechanic

BY DOUG CENKO

My mama is
a lot of things...

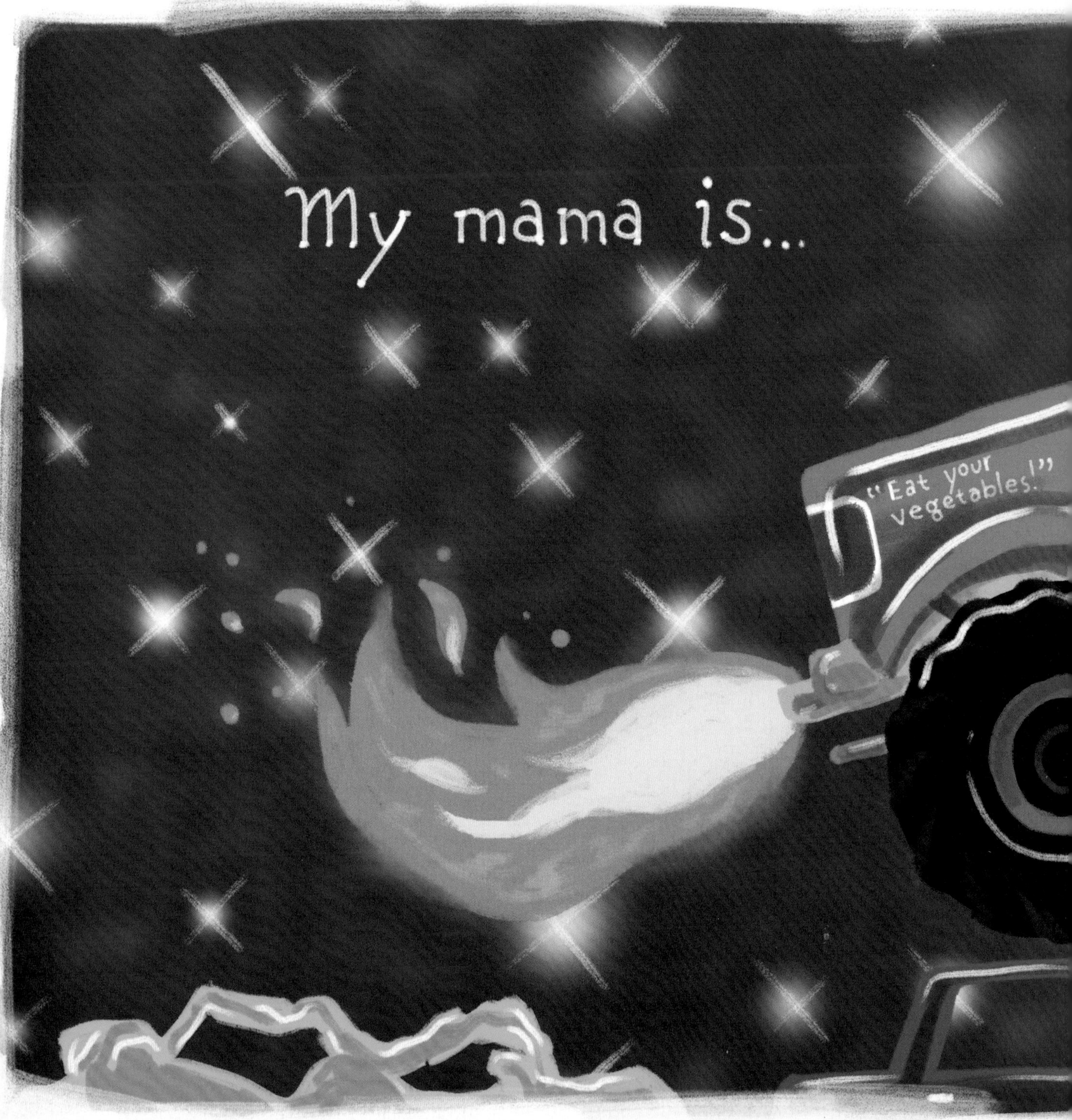
My mama is...
"Eat your vegetables!"

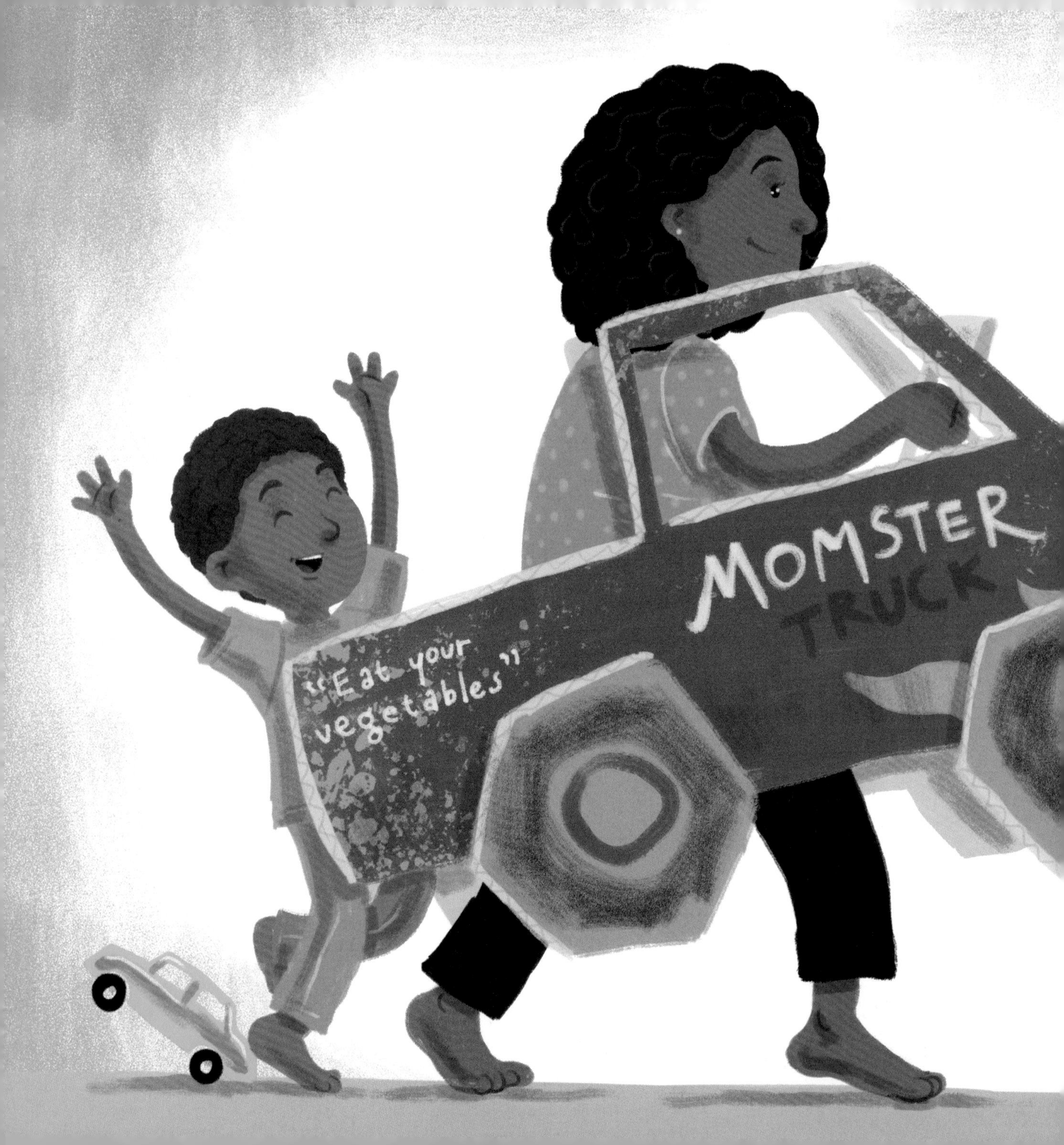
"Eat your vegetables"
MOMSTER
TRUCK

A MONSTER TRUCK DRIVER!

My mama is...

My mama is...

A QUARTERBACK !

A TREASURE HUNTER!

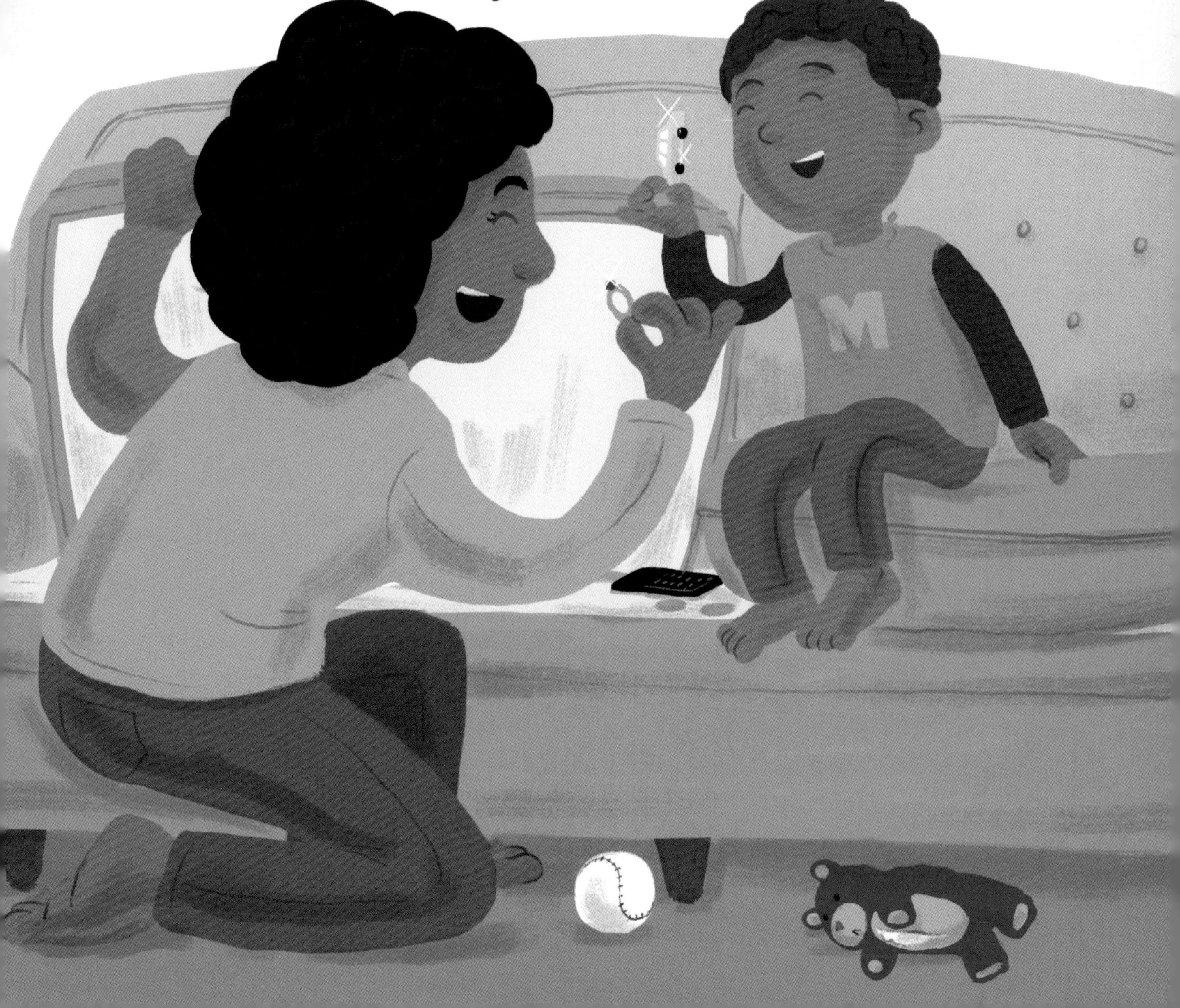

My mama is...

A SURGEON!

A HOT LAVA RESCUER!

But, what I like **BEST** about my mama...

is that she's...

My mama!

THE END